The Space Fort

Story by Michèle Dufresne
Illustrations by Tatjana Mai-Wyss

PIONEER VALLEY EDUCATIONAL PRESS, INC.

"Come on," said Galaxy Girl.
"Let's make a little fort
in this tree."

"Good idea!" said Spaceboy.

Spaceboy and Galaxy Girl
worked and worked.
They worked and worked and worked.
They made a little fort
in the tree.

"Let's go up into the fort,"
said Galaxy Girl.
Spaceboy and Galaxy Girl went up.
Spacedog and Spacecat went up, too.

"Look! A fort!" said a Spacekid.
"Can I come up?"

"Yes," said Spaceboy. "Come on up."

"Let's make a **big** fort,"
said Galaxy Girl.

"Good idea," said Spaceboy.